Dear Parent:

Congratulations! Your child is taking the first steps on an exciting journey. The destination? Independent reading!

STEP INTO READING® will help your child get there. The program offers books at five levels that accompany children from their first attempts at reading to reading success. Each step includes fun stories, fiction and nonfiction, and colorful art. There are also Step into Reading Sticker Books, Step into Reading Math Readers, and Step into Reading Phonics Readers— a complete literacy program with something to interest every child.

Learning to Read, Step by Step!

Ready to Read Preschool–Kindergarten
• big type and easy words • rhyme and rhythm • picture clues
For children who know the alphabet and are eager to begin reading.

Reading with Help Preschool–Grade 1
• basic vocabulary • short sentences • simple stories
For children who recognize familiar words and sound out new words with help.

Reading on Your Own Grades 1–3
• engaging characters • easy-to-follow plots • popular topics
For children who are ready to read on their own.

Reading Paragraphs Grades 2–3
• challenging vocabulary • short paragraphs • exciting stories
For newly independent readers who read simple sentences with confidence.

Ready for Chapters Grades 2–4
• chapters • longer paragraphs • full-color art
For children who want to take the plunge into chapter books but still like colorful pictures.

STEP INTO READING® is designed to give every child a successful reading experience. The grade levels are only guides. Children can progress through the steps at their own speed, developing confidence in their reading, no matter what their grade.

Remember, a lifetime love of reading starts with a single step!

Text copyright © 2004 by Marilyn Sadler. Illustrations copyright © 2004 by Roger Bollen. All rights reserved under International and Pan-American Copyright Conventions. Published in the United States by Random House Children's Books, a division of Random House, Inc., New York, and simultaneously in Canada by Random House of Canada Limited, Toronto.

www.stepintoreading.com

Educators and librarians, for a variety of teaching tools, visit us at www.randomhouse.com/teachers

Library of Congress Cataloging-in-Publication Data
Sadler, Marilyn.
P. J. Funnybunny's bag of tricks / by Marilyn Sadler ; illustrated by Roger Bollen.
   p.   cm. — (Step into reading. A step 2 book)
SUMMARY: P. J. studies and practices to perform a magic show for his family and friends but afterward no one seems to be interested in his tricks, so he shows them the best trick of all.
ISBN 0-375-82444-8 (trade) — ISBN 0-375-92444-2 (lib. bdg.)
[1. Magic tricks—Fiction. 2. Rabbits—Fiction.]
I. Bollen, Roger, ill. II. Title. III. Series: Step into reading. Step 2 book.
PZ7.S1239 Pack 2004 [E]—dc21 2002152690

Printed in the United States of America First Edition 10 9 8 7 6 5 4 3 2 1

STEP INTO READING, RANDOM HOUSE, and the Random House colophon are registered trademarks of Random House, Inc.

P. J. Funnybunny's Bag of Tricks

By Marilyn Sadler
Illustrated by Roger Bollen

Random House New York

One day,

Mr. Funnybunny

brought home

a surprise for P. J.

It was a magic kit!

"Thanks, Dad!"

said P. J.

P. J. opened the box.

He found

a magic wand

and a red scarf.

He found

a top hat

and a magic book.

"Practice! Practice!
Practice!" P. J. read.

P. J. looked in the mirror.

He practiced, practiced,

practiced.

"Now I will have
a magic show!"
said P. J.

P. J. snapped
a carrot in half.
He dropped it
into his hat.
He waved his
magic wand.

P. J. pulled out

the carrot.

"Ta-da!" he said.

The carrot was whole!

P. J. held up
a glass of milk.
He covered it
with his red scarf.
He waved his
magic wand.

He pulled away
the scarf.
"Ta-da!" said P. J.
The milk was blue!

P. J. did trick
after trick.
He read
his mother's mind.

He made Honey Bunny's
doll float.

He made Potts Pig's
candy bar go away.

P. J. asked his mother,
"Do you want me to read
your mind again?"
But his mother wanted
to read a book.

He asked Honey Bunny,
"Do you want me to make
your doll float?"
But Honey Bunny wanted
to have a tea party.

He asked Potts Pig,
"Do you want me to
make your candy bar
go away?"
But Potts Pig went away.

P. J. was mad.

"I will show you
the biggest trick
of all!" he said.

Poof!

P. J. was gone.

There was a knock
at the door.
It was Grandma
and Grandpa!
"Where is P. J.?"
they asked.

His mother looked
under his bed.

His father looked
in his closet.

"Where could he be?"
his brothers and
sister asked.

BOING!

P. J.'s top hat hopped
across the floor.

Out jumped P. J.!
"Ta-da!" he said.

The Funnybunnys were
happy to see P. J.!
This was his
best trick of all!

Here is a trick for you to try.

1. Fold a piece of paper over
   a coin from left to right . . .

from top to bottom . . .   and from right to left.

2. Hold the paper up with the
   open end facing down. The
   coin will fall into your sleeve.

3. Open the paper.
   Say, "Ta-da! The coin is gone!"